TRANG NGUYEN   JEET ZDUNG

SAVING SORYA
Chang and the Sun Bear

MACMILLAN CHILDREN'S BOOKS

TO DAISY, LINH ĐAN,
AND ALL YOUNG
ANIMAL LOVERS
EVERYWHERE.

HELLO READERS,

MY NAME IS TRANG AND I AM A VIETNAMESE WILDLIFE CONSERVATIONIST. BEFORE YOU READ THIS BOOK, I'D LIKE TO TELL YOU MORE ABOUT IT. *SAVING SORYA* IS THE STORY OF CHANG, A LITTLE GIRL WITH A HUGE DREAM TO PROTECT AND CONSERVE THE LIVES OF WILD ANIMALS WHO ARE BEING PUSHED TOWARDS EXTINCTION BY HUMANS. CHANG WORKS HARD TO FOLLOW HER DREAMS, AND SHE IGNORES PEOPLE WHO THINK WILDLIFE CONSERVATION IS NOT A GOOD CAREER FOR HER.

WHEN CHANG MEETS SORYA, A SMALL AND TIMID SUN BEAR, SHE DECIDES THAT SHE WILL DO EVERYTHING SHE CAN TO RETURN SORYA TO THE RAINFOREST. THIS IS A STORY INSPIRED BY REAL CHARACTERS AND EVENTS: CHANG IS BASED ON ME. MY LIFE CHANGED WHEN I ACCIDENTALLY WITNESSED A MOON BEAR WHOSE BILE WAS BEING EXTRACTED. AT THAT MOMENT, I DECIDED THERE WAS NOTHING ELSE I WANTED TO DO MORE THAN BECOME A CONSERVATIONIST AND CREATE A BETTER, SAFER WORLD FOR WILD ANIMALS.

SORYA IS A REAL SUN BEAR WHO WAS RESCUED FROM THE ILLEGAL BEAR TRADE BY A WONDERFUL ORGANIZATION IN SOUTHEAST ASIA CALLED FREE THE BEARS. BUT HER JOURNEY IN THIS BOOK IS BASED ON THE STORY OF A MOON BEAR NAMED POLA. POLA WAS RESCUED IN 2008 AND REINTRODUCED TO THE WILD.

IN READING THIS STORY, YOU'LL LEARN MORE ABOUT AN AMAZING CREATURE - THE SUN BEAR - AND ITS IMPORTANT ROLE IN THE FOREST, AS WELL AS THE LIFE-SAVING CONSERVATION WORK BEING CARRIED OUT TO PROTECT THESE ANIMALS AND THEIR FOREST HOME. I HOPE THIS STORY GIVES YOU THE ENCOURAGEMENT AND INSPIRATION TO FOLLOW YOUR OWN DREAMS, WHATEVER THEY MAY BE, AND TO NEVER GIVE UP.

TRANG NGUYEN

THIS IS THE RAINFOREST, ON A MORNING WITHOUT RAIN.

IT IS FILLED WITH WILD CREATURES.

OOF!

SORYA, NO!

BAD BEAR, SORYA!

SNIFF!
SLURP!

OH, SORYA - MY NOTEBOOK'S ALL WET!

GRRR

SORYA IS A LOVELY LITTLE SUN BEAR.

WHAT ARE YOU SNIFFING AT?

YOU ARE NOT A DOG!

SLURP

YOU'RE A WILD BEAR, REMEMBER?

SHE WAS CAPTURED AND SENT TO A BEAR BILE FARM WHEN SHE WAS A BABY.

GO AND LOOK FOR FOOD YOURSELF!

HOW ARE YOU GOING TO LIVE IN THE FOREST IF YOU KEEP WAITING FOR ME TO FEED YOU?

MY JOB IS TO BRING HER BACK TO THE FOREST AND TEACH HER HOW TO LIVE ON HER OWN.

GRRR

EEK!

A TOAD

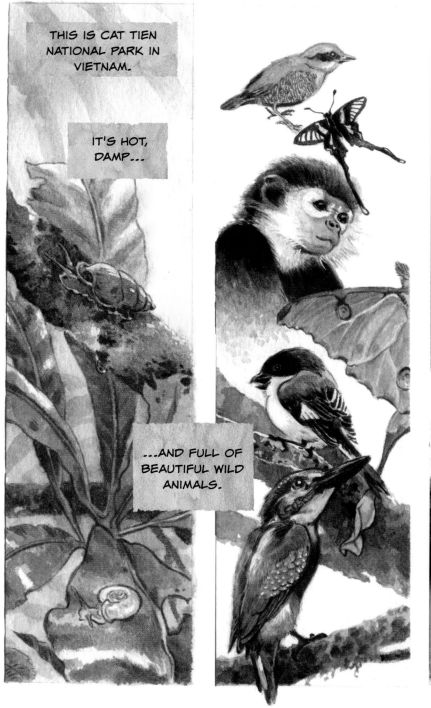

THIS IS CAT TIEN NATIONAL PARK IN VIETNAM.

IT'S HOT, DAMP...

...AND FULL OF BEAUTIFUL WILD ANIMALS.

IT IS ALSO HOME TO VICIOUS MOSQUITOES.

THEY CAN CAUSE A DEADLY DISEASE CALLED MALARIA.

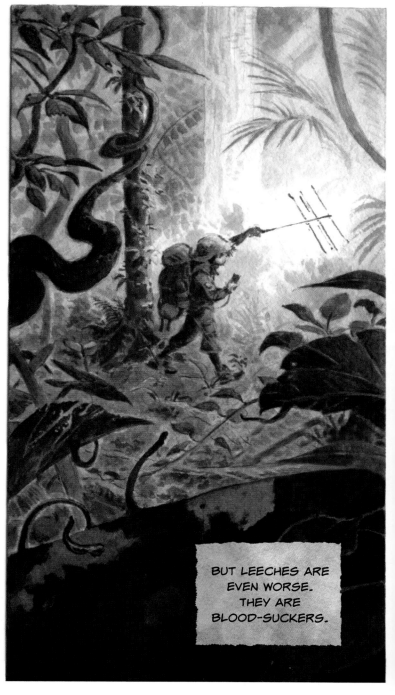

BUT LEECHES ARE EVEN WORSE. THEY ARE BLOOD-SUCKERS.

LEECHES CRAWL...

...EVERY-WHERE!

My natural insect repellent scares the mosquitoes and leeches off.

organic lime and lemongrass

apply here

apply here

FLICK...

I ALSO USE A STICK TO FLICK THE LEECHES AWAY.

CRACK!

SCRATCH...

SNIFF...

SCRATCH...

SNIFF...

SLURP!

PANT PANT!

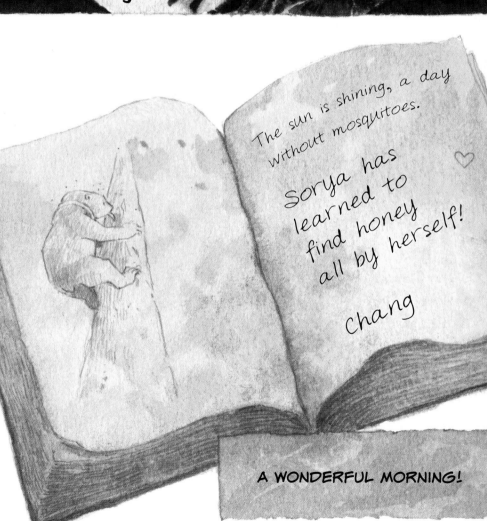

The sun is shining, a day without mosquitoes.

Sorya has learned to find honey all by herself!

Chang

A WONDERFUL MORNING!

I'VE WANTED TO BECOME A CONSERVATIONIST SINCE I WAS EIGHT YEARS OLD. IT ALL BEGAN WHEN I WAS WALKING BACK FROM SCHOOL WITH A FRIEND...

WE HEARD A TERRIBLE NOISE COMING FROM INSIDE A HOUSE.

UHH

UHH

UHH

WE CREPT CLOSER. TO OUR SURPRISE, WE COULD HEAR VOICES INSIDE.

?

EWW! WHAT'S THAT SMELL?!

WE PEERED INSIDE AND SAW SOMETHING AWFUL.

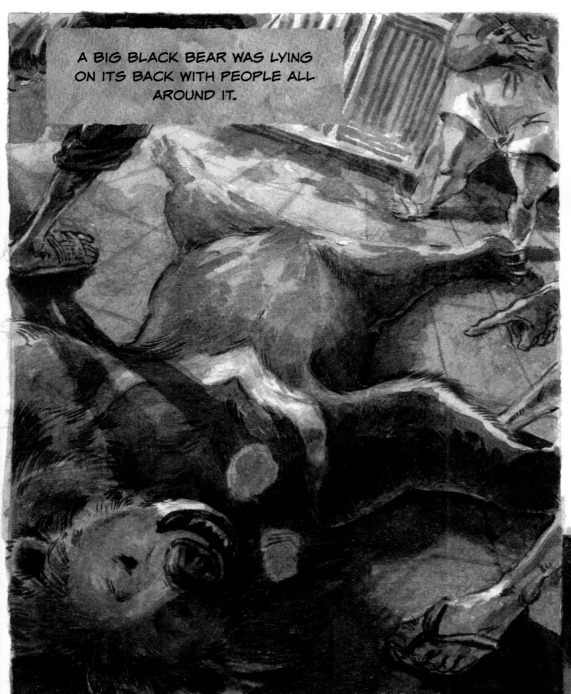

A BIG BLACK BEAR WAS LYING ON ITS BACK WITH PEOPLE ALL AROUND IT.

THE TERRIBLE SOUND WE HAD HEARD EARLIER WAS THE BEAR CRYING.

UHH

A MAN WAS STANDING ABOVE IT HOLDING A GIANT NEEDLE.

NOOOOO!

WE WERE SO FRIGHTENED WE RAN AWAY.

I DIDN'T KNOW IT THEN, BUT MY FRIEND AND I HAD DISCOVERED A BEAR FARM.

THEY WERE TRYING TO REMOVE A FLUID FROM THE BEAR'S BODY, CALLED BILE.

BEAR BILE HAS BEEN USED IN MEDICINE FOR THOUSANDS OF YEARS.

BUT NOW WE HAVE MEDICINE THAT DOESN'T USE IT, AND DOESN'T HURT BEARS.

THAT NIGHT I MADE A PROMISE TO MYSELF. I WOULD NOT LET HUMANS ABUSE BEARS, OR ANY OTHER WILD ANIMALS, IF I COULD STOP THEM.

SO, THE VERY NEXT DAY,
I DECIDED TO BECOME A
WILDLIFE CONSERVATIONIST.

I HAD HEARD
ABOUT
WILDLIFE
CONSERVATIONISTS
ON TV.
THEY ARE
PEOPLE WHO
PROTECT NATURE ALL
OVER THE WORLD —
IN DESERTS, NEAR
OCEANS, AND EVEN
INSIDE CAVES.

THAT'S WHEN
I REALIZED:
I COULD
PROTECT THE
RAINFOREST
NEAR MY HOME!

WELL, THERE WAS ONE THING STOPPING ME... ALL THE BOOKS I FOUND ABOUT CONSERVATION WERE IN **ENGLISH!**

GRRR! I DON'T UNDERSTAND ANYTHING!

MY ENGLISH IS TERRIBLE.

PEOPLE ALSO HAD A LOT TO SAY ABOUT MY PLAN...

HOW CAN A GIRL LIKE YOU WORK IN THE FOREST?

HA HA HA, SUCH A CHILDISH DREAM.

YOU SHOULD BE REALISTIC. BE A TEACHER OR AN ACCOUNTANT!

ONLY WESTERNERS CAN BE CONSERVATIONISTS. THEY HAVE TIME AND MONEY.

YOU CAN'T EVEN TAKE CARE OF YOURSELF; HOW CAN YOU PROTECT WILD ANIMALS?

A GIRL LIKE YOU SHOULD CONCENTRATE ON SCHOOL, THEN GET MARRIED WHEN YOU GROW UP.

DON'T BE RIDICULOUS!

PEOPLE DON'T DO THAT IN VIETNAM!

AND MY GENDER...

GIRLS ARE SO WEAK! THERE IS NO WAY YOU CAN PROTECT WILD ANIMALS.

PANT PANT PANT PANT PANT PANT

I WANT TO BE A VOLUNTEER AT YOUR ORGANIZATION.

THANK YOU, BUT YOU ARE SO SMALL.

ONLY EIGHT YEARS OLD!

...AND EVEN MY AGE. NO ONE WOULD HIRE ME.

IT WAS AMAZING WORKING AS AN ANIMAL-RESCUE VOLUNTEER IN CAT TIEN NATIONAL PARK. I MADE FRIENDS WITH ANIMAL LOVERS FROM ALL OVER THE WORLD AND LEARNED A LOT ABOUT CONSERVATION.

WILDLIFE RESCUE AND CONSERVATION CENTRE

TOGETHER WE PREPARED FOOD FOR ALL THE CREATURES LIVING THERE. THEY WERE OFTEN SICK AND INJURED.

WE CLEANED UP BEAR POOP AND MADE HAMMOCKS FOR THE BEARS TO USE.

THE ANIMALS WERE RESCUED FROM POACHERS - PEOPLE WHO CAPTURE AND HURT WILD ANIMALS BEFORE THEY SELL THEM.

WE ALSO HELPED PANGOLINS - ONE OF THE MOST ENDANGERED ANIMALS IN THE WORLD.

I NEVER FORGOT THE BEAR I SAW ON THE FLOOR OF THAT BILE FARM. SO I VOLUNTEERED AT FREE THE BEARS.

IT WAS AN ORGANIZATION THAT RESCUED BEARS FROM BILE FARMS ALL OVER SOUTHEAST ASIA.

FREE THE BEARS

THE POOR BEARS WERE FINALLY FREE FROM THEIR TERRIBLE, TINY CAGES.

ONE DAY, A TINY TWO-WEEK-OLD BEAR CUB ARRIVED AT THE CENTRE.

HER NAME WAS SORYA, MEANING 'SUN' IN VIETNAMESE.

SORYA WAS CAPTURED FROM A FOREST IN LAOS. WE DON'T KNOW WHAT HAPPENED TO HER MOTHER, BUT WE GUESSED THAT POACHERS HAD GOT HER.

SORYA WAS VERY DIFFERENT FROM MISA.

THERE ARE TWO SPECIES OF BEAR IN VIETNAM:

THE MOON BEAR:

THE SUN BEAR:

long hair

a white or yellow V shape on its chest

a yellow or orange U shape on its chest

small ears

short and smooth hair

ENGLISH NAME: moon bear
SCIENTIFIC NAME: ursus thibetanus
ALSO KNOWN AS: Asian black bear, Asiatic black bear, Himalayan black bear.
They are between 1.3 and 1.9m tall with long, sharp claws.

ENGLISH NAME: sun bear
SCIENTIFIC NAME: helarctos malayanus
ALSO KNOWN AS: honey bear, Malaysian sun bear.
The sun bear is smaller than the moon bear, at only 1.2m tall.
They are the smallest bear in the bear family and they are only found in Southeast Asia.

THERE ARE EIGHT SPECIES
OF BEAR IN THE WORLD:

PANDA

MOON BEAR

SLOTH BEAR

SPECTACLED
BEAR

SUN BEAR

AMERICAN BLACK BEAR

POLAR BEAR

BROWN
BEAR

I LEARNED EVERYTHING
I COULD ABOUT SUN BEARS...

BIRDS MUST BE ABLE TO FLY...

...AND BEARS MUST BE ABLE TO CLIMB!

GOOD CLIMBERS: THEY SPEND MORE TIME IN TREES THAN ANY OTHER BEAR SPECIES.

OMNIVORES: THEY EAT BOTH ANIMALS AND PLANTS – ANYTHING FROM EGGS, HONEY, FRUITS AND ROOTS TO INSECTS, REPTILES, BIRDS AND ANTS.

SUN BEARS ALSO LIKE COCONUTS! THEY USE THEIR STRONG CLAWS TO TEAR THEM APART.

AGILE FEET: SHARP CLAWS CURVED LIKE HOOKS. THE BOTTOM OF THEIR PAWS DON'T HAVE ANY FUR.

THEIR FEET POINT INWARDS, SO THEY HAVE A VERY FUNNY WALK!

EVEN THOUGH ALL BEARS BELONG IN THE WILD, I LEARNED THAT NOT ALL BEARS, ONCE THEY ARE CAPTURED BY HUMANS, CAN RETURN.

LIKE MISA.

MISA IS OLD AND SICK. SHE HAS BEEN KEPT IN TINY CAGES FOR TOO LONG AND DOESN'T KNOW HOW TO FEND FOR HERSELF.

MISA MUST BE TAKEN CARE OF.

BEARS LIKE MISA LIVE IN CAPTIVITY
FOR THE REST OF THEIR LIVES.
BUT AT FREE THE BEARS, THEY ARE ABLE
TO LIVE IN A SMALL, PROTECTED PART
OF THE NATIONAL PARK, WHERE THEY
FEEL LIKE THEY ARE IN THE WILD.

SHE WAS SMALL, BUT YOUNG AND HEALTHY WHEN WE RESCUED HER.

SHE HAD A GOOD CHANCE OF LEARNING TO FEND FOR HERSELF AND RETURNING TO THE FOREST WHEN SHE WAS OLDER.

SINCE SORYA LOST HER MOTHER, I WAS IN CHARGE OF TEACHING HER SURVIVAL SKILLS, SUCH AS...

...FORAGING AND HUNTING FOR FOOD,

FRESH WATER,

AND A SAFE PLACE TO SLEEP AT NIGHT.

LIKE SOME CUBS WITHOUT MOTHERS, SORYA ALSO DEVELOPED A HABIT OF SUCKING ON HER TOES AND FINGERS.

IT WAS CUTE AT FIRST, BUT EVERY TIME SORYA DID THIS...

SLURP! SUCK!

OH NO! YOUR PAWS ARE BLEEDING!

...SHE'D BREAK THE SKIN AROUND HER TOENAILS AND HURT HERSELF.

Rescued bears often behave strangely.

Some walk back and forth, like they are still inside invisible cages.

Some are covered in scabs, from where they have rubbed their bodies on the bars of their cages.

Some of them don't have fur anymore because of stress or a skin condition that hasn't been treated in time.

Some shake their heads constantly.

These are all signs that some bears can't return to the wild. They've been suffering for too long, and wouldn't be able to take care of themselves.

THEIR BEHAVIOUR WAS DUE TO MONTHS OR YEARS OF BEING KEPT IN TINY CAGES WHERE THEY COULD NOT MOVE OR STAND. HUMANS HAD BEEN CONSTANTLY EXTRACTING THEIR BILE, AND NOW THE BEARS COULDN'T FORGET THAT PAIN – OR THEIR FEAR.

THIS WAS SO TERRIBLE.

I WILL HELP SORYA TO RETURN TO THE WILD!

AT THE BEAR RESCUE CENTRE

IN THE EARLY MORNING...

...WE PREPARED FOOD FOR BEARS.

HEY!

BUT OTHER ANIMALS CAME FOR THEIR SHARE, TOO!

YAY! YOU GOT IT, SORYA!

HA HA! YOU ARE SO CUTE!

EACH DAY I LEFT SORYA'S FOOD IN DIFFERENT PLACES SO SHE'D HAVE TO FIND IT HERSELF.

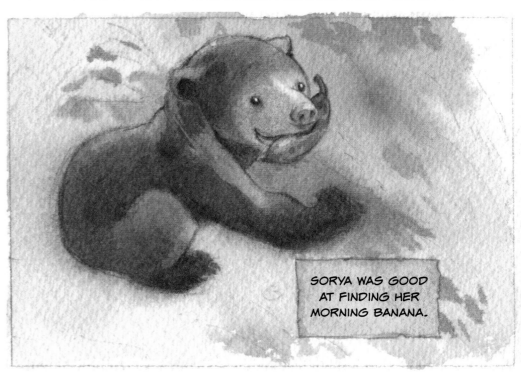

SORYA WAS GOOD AT FINDING HER MORNING BANANA.

?

BUT BULLIES TRIED TO TAKE IT FROM HER!

OH NO! THE OTHER BEAR GOT THE BANANA!

GRRRRR

TAKE IT BACK, SORYA.

BE BRAVE!

BUT SORYA WAS TOO SCARED.

THE NEXT FOREST WAS BEAUTIFUL.

I WAS VERY EXCITED, BUT THEN...

...I DISCOVERED A DAM - A HUMAN-MADE BARRIER USED TO CONTROL WATER.

DURING THE RAINY SEASON, THE DAM WAS OPENED, ALLOWING WATER TO FLOOD THE FOREST.

MANY WILD ANIMALS DROWNED BECAUSE OF THESE FLOODS.

SORYA COULDN'T LIVE THERE.

THE FOURTH FOREST WASN'T A FOREST AT ALL.

IT WAS A CONSTRUCTION SITE, WHERE HOTELS, SHOPPING CENTRES, GOLF COURSES, AND OTHER BUILDINGS WERE BEING BUILT.

SORYA COULDN'T LIVE THERE EITHER.

WAS THERE ANYWHERE FOR HER TO LIVE?

IT WAS SO...

...QUIET.

I WAS SURPRISED BECAUSE A LIVING FOREST IS USUALLY VERY NOISY, FILLED WITH THE SOUNDS OF WILDLIFE.

FINALLY, I WORKED OUT WHY THERE WAS NO NOISE:

SNARE TRAPS.

I RAN AS FAST AS I COULD BACK TO THE CENTRE TO GET HELP.

THE OTHER CONSERVATIONISTS AND I VISITED THE VILLAGE NEAR THE FOREST TO MEET THE LOCAL PEOPLE.

THEY TOLD US THAT MANY PEOPLE FROM OTHER PARTS OF THE COUNTRY CAME THERE TO HUNT ANIMALS...

...AND SELL THEM IN THE CITIES.

MANY WILD ANIMALS AND PLANTS ARE THREATENED WITH EXTINCTION DUE TO HUMAN DEMAND.

SMALL ANIMALS LIKE SQUIRRELS, BIRDS AND LORISES ARE CAUGHT AND SOLD AS PETS, OR KILLED AND MADE INTO PRODUCTS.

EVEN PLANTS LIKE ORCHIDS HAVE BEEN DISAPPEARING FROM THE FOREST.

FREE THE BEARS OFFICERS AND I ORGANIZED TRAINING AND WORKSHOPS FOR THE VILLAGERS.

WE GAVE THEM PROTECTIVE GEAR, LIKE FIELD SHOES AND CLOTHING.

FREE THE BEARS EVEN EMPLOYED THEM TO REMOVE SNARE TRAPS AND PATROL THE FOREST.

WITHOUT SNARE TRAPS,

WILD ANIMALS STARTED
TO RETURN.

AND WHEN THE FOREST BEGAN TO FILL AGAIN
WITH THE SOUNDS OF WILDLIFE...

...I KNEW SORYA COULD
LIVE THERE.

DURING THIS TIME, SORYA HAD GROWN UP.

SHE WAS MUCH BIGGER THAN SHE USED TO BE, AND COULD EVEN USE HER CLAWS TO BREAK OPEN COCONUTS, HER FAVOURITE FOOD!

BEFORE, SORYA HAD BEEN TIMID, AND WAS CONSTANTLY BULLIED BY BIGGER BEARS. NOW, SHE COULD STAND UP FOR HERSELF, AND PROTECT HER FOOD AND SLEEPING NEST.

THERE WERE STILL THINGS FOR SORYA TO LEARN, BUT I KNEW SHE WAS READY FOR HER NEW HOME.

STAY STILL, SORYA.
LET ME PUT THIS TRACKING
COLLAR ON YOU.

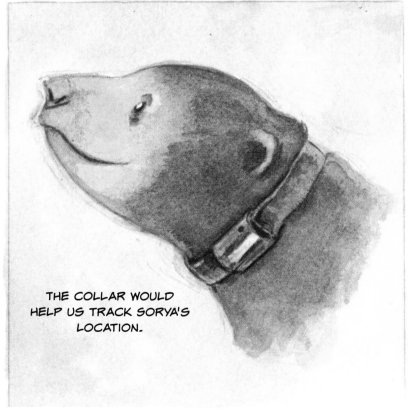

THE COLLAR WOULD
HELP US TRACK SORYA'S
LOCATION.

UHH

DON'T BE
SCARED,
SORYA.
YOU'RE
ALMOST
HOME!

HERE, YOU WALK FIRST — I'LL FOLLOW YOU.

UHH.

OH, THAT'S JUST A LIZARD, SORYA.

makha
—tae
tree

aXlewood
fruit →

still
so shy

Sorya loves swimming
and playing in the
water.

A rainy day

Sorya watches
a bee on a
crape
myrtle
flower.

She tries
to eat a new
plant now
and then.

Wild bear cubs
learn what is good
to eat by smelling their
mother's breath. But
baby bears like Sorya,
who were separated
from their mothers,
have to try everything.
If it doesn't taste good,
they spit it out.

Even though
Sorya is
getting used
to the forest,

she still sleeps
by me at
night.

CROAKKK

CROOAAAKkk

ONE NIGHT, THE SOUND OF A FROG CAUGHT SORYA'S ATTENTION.

CROOAAAKkk

SHE WAS HUNGRY.

SHE WANTED ME TO FEED HER, BUT I WAS TOO TIRED, SO I PRETENDED TO BE ASLEEP.

WHOOSH!!

SORYA TRIED CATCHING THE FROG...

...BUT MISSED,

GRRR

AND MISSED AGAIN,

GRRR

SPLASH!

GRRR GRRR GRRR GRRR

GRRR!!

AND AGAIN.

THE FROG DISAPPEARED.

BUT THEN...

THAT'S IT, SORYA! **COME ON!**

...SORYA FOUND A REALLY BIG TERMITE NEST.

QUICKLY, SHE USED HER STRONG PAWS AND SHARP CLAWS TO DIG INTO IT.

AND STRETCHED HER LOOOOOONG TONGUE INSIDE.

A SUN BEAR'S TONGUE CAN BE AS LONG AS 25CM!

THAT DAY, SORYA PROVED THAT SHE WAS A REAL WILD BEAR, DOING THINGS SHE COULD NOT HAVE DONE BEFORE!

AND MET SOME AMAZING WILD ANIMALS ALONG THE WAY,

SUCH AS GAURS.

THE LOCAL PEOPLE CALLED THEM MIN. THEY WERE SOME OF THE BIGGEST AND STRONGEST ANIMALS IN THE PARK.

THIS GAUR WAS VIGILANT! I KNEW I'D BETTER STAY AWAY FROM HIM.

SOMETIMES, SORYA GOT AHEAD OF ME, AND I HAD TO USE THE TRACKER ON HER COLLAR TO FIND HER.

SHE COULD MAKE HER WAY THROUGH THICK BAMBOO, BUT I COULDN'T.

OUCH!

SORYA HAD BECOME MUCH BRAVER, AND WAS STARTING TO EXPLORE BY HERSELF.

THE JOURNEY
WAS TOUGH, BUT THE
DISCOVERIES WE MADE
TOGETHER WERE
WORTH IT.

Sun bears like Sorya are called the 'doctors' and 'gardeners' of the rainforest. They make the forest healthier and help it in lots of ways.

The fruit seeds they spread through their poop grow into new plants.

They eat termites, controlling pest populations.

Sun bears break up rotten logs, which turns them into soil faster.

Lots of animals benefit from the things Sorya does!

SORYA WAS HAPPIER NOW, IN HER NEW HOME.

SUN BEARS ARE ALSO CALLED HONEY BEARS BECAUSE THEY'RE GOOD AT CLIMBING TREES AND USE THEIR STRONG SENSE OF SMELL TO LOCATE HONEY.

SORYA WAS A TRUE HONEY BEAR NOW, FINDING FOOD ALL BY HERSELF!

AT NIGHT, SHE USED TO FIND ME...

...AND WE'D SLEEP UNDER THE STARS.

But now, my dear Sorya is a lot more confident.

She makes her own nest in the trees and sleeps there by herself.

Sorya doesn't depend on me like she used to.

But even after living by herself for some time, she'll come by to say hello.

She's learned to stay away from other humans.

So I know she'll stay away from poachers, too.

ONE MORNING, AFTER MONTHS OF NO TROUBLE...

...SORYA'S TRACKER FELL OFF.

AFTER SEARCHING HIGH AND LOW, I FOUND A SUN-BEAR SIGN - CLAW MARKS IN A NEARBY TREE!

BUT THE MARKS WERE NOT SORYA'S. THIS BEAR WAS MUCH TALLER THAN HER.

THIS IS A FRESH MARK.

I STARTED TO GET WORRIED!

WHAT IF SORYA HAD WANDERED INTO ANOTHER BEAR'S TERRITORY?

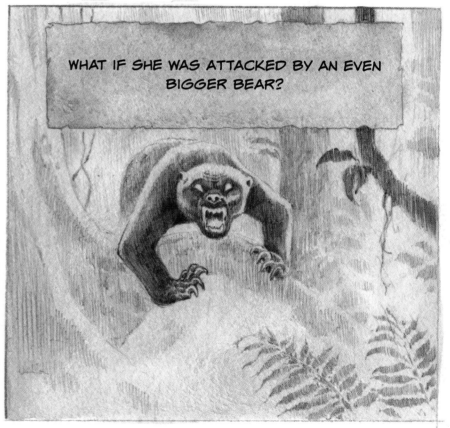

WHAT IF SHE WAS ATTACKED BY AN EVEN BIGGER BEAR?

GRRR!

SORYA?!

AT FIRST THEY WERE CAUTIOUS WITH EACH OTHER, AND ATE AS MANY FIGS AS THEY COULD WITHOUT MAKING EYE CONTACT.

IT WAS ALMOST LIKE THEY WERE IN AN EATING COMPETITION.

BUT AFTER A WHILE, THEIR LOVE OF FOOD OVERCAME THEIR FEAR OF ONE ANOTHER.

AFTER THE FEAST, SORYA AND HER NEW FRIEND FELL ASLEEP UNDER THE FIG TREE.

THAT'S WHEN I REALIZED...

...IT WAS TIME TO SAY GOODBYE TO SORYA.

BUT IT WAS HARD TO WALK AWAY.

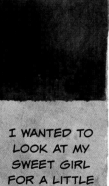

I WANTED TO LOOK AT MY SWEET GIRL FOR A LITTLE LONGER.

MY NAME IS CHANG.

I AM A WILDLIFE
CONSERVATIONIST.

MY AIM WAS TO FIND SORYA
A HOME, AND HELP HER TO
LIVE IN THE FOREST...

...WILD AND FREE.

THE END

A MESSAGE FROM TRANG AND JEET:

WE WOULD LIKE TO SEND OUR SINCERE
THANKS TO MATT HUNT, BRIAN CRUDGE,
MARION SCHNEIDER, AND FREE THE BEARS
ORGANIZATION, WHO GAVE US A WONDERFUL
OPPORTUNITY TO CREATE THIS BOOK. PLEASE
VISIT THE FREE THE BEARS WEBSITE AND
SUPPORT THEIR WORK!

WWW.FREETHEBEARS.ORG

ILLUSTRATOR'S NOTE:

I WOULD LIKE TO THANK TRANG NGUYEN, THE BRAVE AND KIND-HEARTED CONSERVATIONIST, A FRIEND OF MINE. I WOULD NOT HAVE BEEN ABLE TO CREATE THIS WORK WITHOUT HER STORIES, HER KNOWLEDGE, AND HER REAL-LIFE EXPERIENCES. THANKS TO TRANG, I HAD THE CHANCE TO VOLUNTEER AT WILDLIFE RESCUE CENTRES AND DO FIELDWORK (THANKS MATT HUNT FOR SUPPORTING ME EVEN THOUGH WE'VE NEVER HAD THE CHANCE TO MEET). I SINCERELY APPRECIATE BRIAN CRUDGE AND MARION SCHNEIDER, THE TWO EXPERTS ON BEARS WHO SHARED THEIR VALUABLE KNOWLEDGE OF BEAR CONSERVATION. IT WAS A PRIVILEGE TO WORK WITH THEM. I WOULD ALSO LIKE TO THANK THE STAFF AND VOLUNTEERS AT FREE THE BEARS RESCUE CENTRE IN CAT TIEN NATIONAL PARK, VIETNAM, AND PHNOM TAMAO WILDLIFE RESCUE CENTRE IN CAMBODIA.

MY GRATITUDE GOES TO PHUONG AN (PAN) AND NGUYET HANG (MOCHI MUN), MY TWO LOVELY AND DEDICATED ASSISTANTS. BESIDE THE HARD WORK OF SEARCHING, CATEGORIZING, DRAWING, AND TAKING DETAILED NOTES ON PLANTS NATIVE TO VIETNAM, THEY ALSO PROVIDED ME WITH DRAWING PAPER AND FOOD WHEN TIMES WERE TOUGH.

THANKS TO TA LAN HANH FOR INTRODUCING ME TO LINH PHAN, THE TALENTED DESIGNER WHO WAS FULLY DEVOTED TO THE PROJECT.

AND ONCE AGAIN, THANK YOU TO TRANG FOR HER PATIENCE.

JEET ZDUNG

ABOUT THE AUTHOR:

TRANG NGUYEN IS A VIETNAMESE WILDLIFE CONSERVATIONIST, ENVIRONMENTAL ACTIVIST AND WRITER, KNOWN FOR HER CONSERVATION WORK IN TACKLING THE ILLEGAL WILDLIFE TRADE IN AFRICA AND ASIA. TRANG GRADUATED WITH HER PHD IN BIODIVERSITY MANAGEMENT AT THE UNIVERSITY OF KENT, ENGLAND, RESEARCHING THE IMPACT ON AFRICAN WILDLIFE OF WILD ANIMAL-PART USE IN TRADITIONAL ASIAN MEDICINE. IN 2018, TRANG WAS FEATURED IN THE DOCUMENTARY FILM *STROOP: JOURNEY INTO THE RHINO HORN WAR*, ALONGSIDE JANE GOODALL. IN 2019, SHE WAS NAMED ON THE BBC'S 100 WOMEN OF 2019 LIST. IN 2020, SHE APPEARED IN THE FORBES 30 UNDER 30 ASIA LIST. TRANG IS THE FOUNDER AND EXECUTIVE DIRECTOR OF WILDACT, AN NGO THAT MONITORS THE ILLEGAL WILDLIFE TRADE MARKETS AND PROVIDES CONSERVATION EDUCATION PROGRAMMES FOR VIETNAMESE YOUTH. SHE IS ALSO A MEMBER OF THE IUCN SSC BEAR SPECIALIST GROUP, WHICH STRIVES TO PROMOTE THE CONSERVATION OF BEARS LIVING IN THEIR NATURAL HABITATS AROUND THE WORLD. *SAVING SORYA: CHANG AND THE SUN BEAR* IS HER FIRST CHILDREN'S BOOK.

ABOUT THE ILLUSTRATOR:

JEET ZDUNG FUSES TRADITIONAL VIETNAMESE ART WITH MANGA, USING PENCILS, WATERCOLOURS, INK AND OTHER DIGITAL MEANS TO CREATE WORKS OF BEAUTY AND INNOVATION. HE HAS WON SEVERAL AWARDS, INCLUDING A SILENT MANGA AUDITION EXCELLENCE AWARD FOR HIS MANGA *STAND UP AND FLY*. *SAVING SORYA: CHANG AND THE SUN BEAR* IS HIS FIRST CHILDREN'S BOOK PUBLISHED IN THE UK AND US. HE LIVES IN HANOI, VIETNAM.

WILDACT IS A NOT-FOR-PROFIT CONSERVATION
ORGANIZATION BASED IN VIETNAM, ESTABLISHED IN 2015.
ITS MISSION IS TO INSPIRE, MOTIVATE AND EMPOWER SOCIETY
AND INDIVIDUALS TO ENGAGE IN THE SCIENCE-BASED
CONSERVATION OF THREATENED SPECIES AND ECOSYSTEMS.

Published 2021 by Macmillan Children's Books
an imprint of Pan Macmillan
The Smithson, 6 Briset Street, London, EC1M 5NR
Associated companies throughout the world
www.panmacmillan.com

EU representative: Macmillan Publishers Ireland Limited,
Mallard Lodge, Lansdowne Village, Dublin 4

ISBN 978-0-7534-4659-1

A CIP catalogue record for this book
is available from the British Library.

1 3 5 7 9 8 6 4 2
1TR/0621/RV/WKT/140MA

Printed in China